BIG BAD BUBBLE

WORDS BY
Adam Rubin

PICTURES BY
Daniel Salmieri

CLARION BOOKS   HOUGHTON MIFFLIN HARCOURT   BOSTON NEW YORK

Clarion Books

215 Park Avenue South

New York, New York 10003

Text copyright © 2014 by Adam Rubin

Illustrations copyright © 2014 by Daniel Salmieri

Clarion Books is an imprint of

Houghton Mifflin Harcourt

Publishing Company.

www.hmhbooks.com

The illustrations were executed in watercolor,

pen and ink, and collage.

The text was set in 15-point Bryant.

Book design by Kerry Martin

Library of Congress Cataloging-in-Publication Data

Rubin, Adam, 1983–

Big bad bubble / by Adam Rubin ; illustrated by

Daniel Salmieri.

pages cm

Summary: With gentle prodding from the narrator

and help from the reader, four monsters are led

to face their greatest fear—bubbles.

ISBN 978-0-544-04549-1 (hardcover)

[1. Bubbles—Fiction. 2. Fear—Fiction.

3. Monsters—Fiction. 4. Humorous stories.]

I. Salmieri, Daniel, 1983– illustrator.

II. Title.

PZ7.R83116Big 2014

[E]—dc23

2013020243

Manufactured in China

SCP 10 9 8 7 6 5 4 3 2 1

4500453744

For the Annoyance: Mick, Jen, and all
my other fearless friends
–A.R.

For Adrienne and Will
–D.S.

YOU may not know this, but when a bubble pops, it doesn't just disappear.

For some reason, all the big, scary monsters are terrified of bubbles.

Froofle, why are you running away?

Yerburt, what's the matter?

Wumpus, stop crying.
(Tell Wumpus to stop crying.)

Turns out, it's all Mogo's fault. When he was little, a chewing-gum bubble attacked his face. Since then, all he can talk about is how dangerous bubbles are.

Bubbles are sneaky. You never hear them coming.

Where there's one bubble, there are many bubbles. They travel in packs.

Summer is the worst time for bubbles. That's when they go into a feeding frenzy.

UNDERSTANDING BUBBLES
A Guided Inquiry
By Dr. Mogo Pogo, PHD

Don't listen to Mogo. He has no idea what he's talking about.

I'll admit it's a bit surprising when a bubble suddenly appears out of nowhere. But that's part of the deal with living in La La Land. On the plus side, doughnuts grow on trees, and the rent is cheap.

FOR RENT
$26 per month

Hey, look! Here comes a bubble now.
Yerburt, stop running around in circles.
You have giant fangs.

Froofle, climb down from that tree.
Look at your claws. You have pointy claws.

Wumpus, get out from under those covers.
You're much too big for that bed anyhow.

Look, here's a bubble. It's just a thin layer of soap and water wrapped around a ball of air. It's soft and delicate. It couldn't hurt a fly.

You could pop it with a little finger.

See?

Yerburt, use your fangs.

Froofle, use your claws.

Wumpus, don't be scared. It's just a teeny,
tiny . . . oh, wait. That's kind of a big one.

He's a goner.

Quiet, Mogo. Go on,
Wumpus. You can do it.
(Tell Wumpus he can do it.)

KABOOM!

See? Mogo doesn't know what he's talking about. There's no reason to be afraid.

Enjoy your bubble gum, Yerburt.

Have fun popping your bubble wrap, Froofle.

Oh, boy, that is a big bath full of bubbles, Wumpus!

(Tell Wumpus to save some water for the fish.)

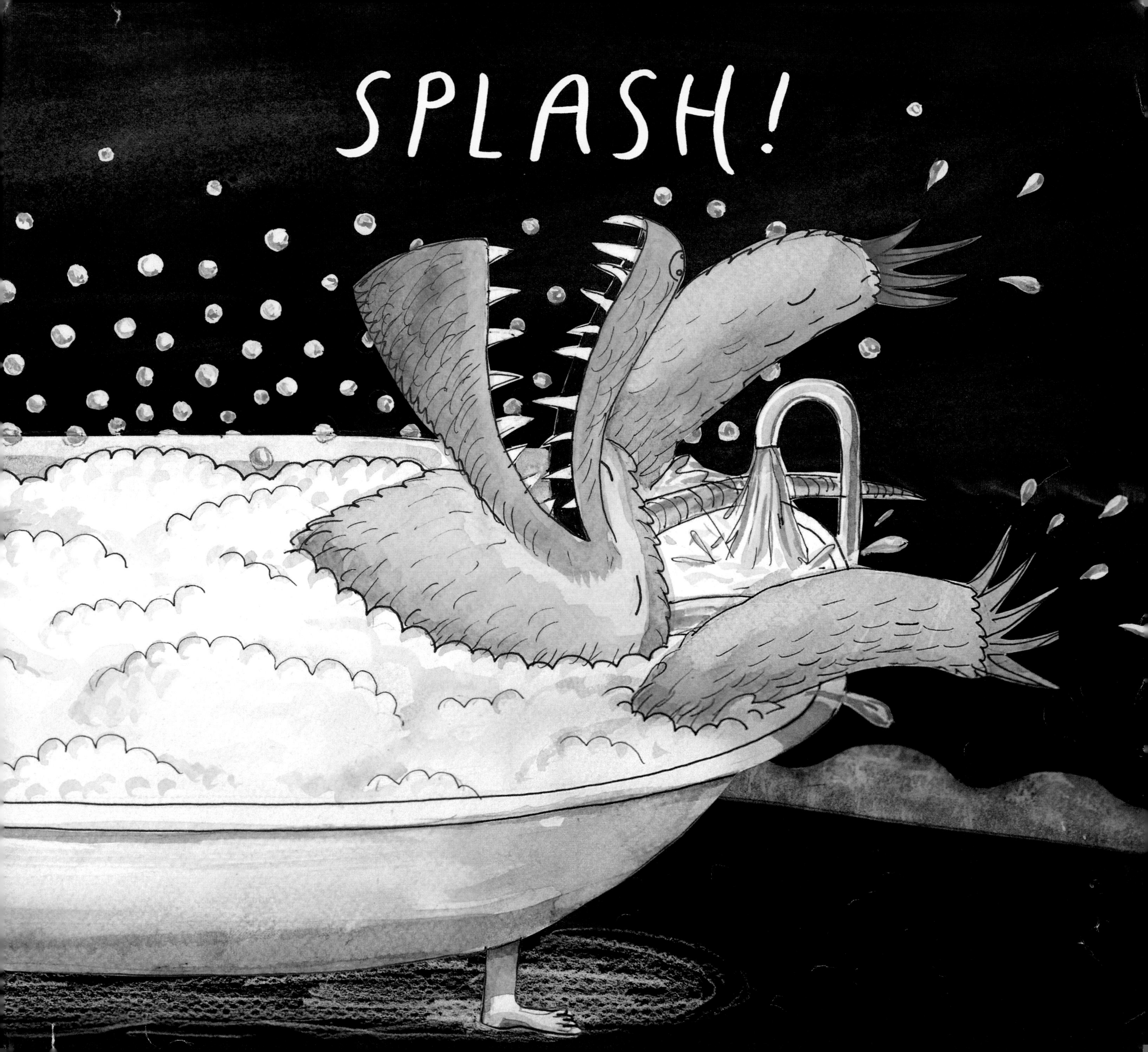
SPLASH!

Fine, maybe bubbles aren't so dangerous after all.
Butterflies, on the other hand...